SCARLET MONSTER LIVES HERE

by Marjorie Weinman Sharmat

Illustrated by Dennis Kendrick

HARPER & ROW, PUBLISHERS
New York, Hagerstown, San Francisco, London

An I CAN READ Book

Library of Congress Cataloging in Publication Data
Sharmat, Marjorie Weinman.
   Scarlet Monster lives here.

   (An I can read book)
   SUMMARY: New in the neighborhood, Scarlet Monster
keeps herself so busy preparing for guests, she
doesn't have time to realize her guests are waiting
to visit.
   [1. Neighborliness—Fiction.   2. Monsters—Fiction]
I. Kendrick, Dennis.   II. Title.
PZ7.S5299Sc 1979   [E]   78-19484
ISBN 0-06-025526-9
ISBN 0-06-025527-7 lib. bdg.

for Mitch
with all my love

M.W.S.

to Fred, Jr.

D.K.

Scarlet Monster

liked her new house.

She unpacked her furniture,

hung her family pictures

of Ma and Pa Monster

and Grandma and Grandpa Monster,

printed her new address

on her stationery,

and got ready for company.

"I can hardly wait

for my new neighbors

to meet me!" she thought.

Scarlet looked out the window.

"I hope they kiss

in this neighborhood.

They will kiss me

or hug me

or even both.

Then they will ask me

to play catch

and go on bike rides

and picnics,

and I will say *yes*!"

Scarlet went to her door.

"Any moment there will be

a knock on it," she said.

Then she thought,

"But what if no one knows I am here?"

Scarlet printed a sign.

She hung it

outside her front door.

UNDER NEW OWNERSHIP.

WELCOME!

"Now everyone will know

that someone wonderful

is living in the neighborhood."

13

Scarlet rushed into her kitchen.

"I will bake some brownies

and pickle some beets

to give to my new friends."

Scarlet baked a dozen brownies

and pickled a bunch of beets.

Then she looked out

her window again.

"Nobody in sight yet," she said.

Scarlet thought about her sign.

"It only says *new*.

It doesn't say *who*."

Scarlet went outside

and took down her sign.

Then she got some paint and a brush

and painted SCARLET MONSTER

in big letters on her mailbox.

"Now everyone and the mailman

will know

that Scarlet Monster lives here."

18

Scarlet went inside

to read a book

about how to make

new friends happy.

Then she closed her book and said,

"Scarlet Monster, you are stupid!

How can anyone come to visit

unless you keep your door open?

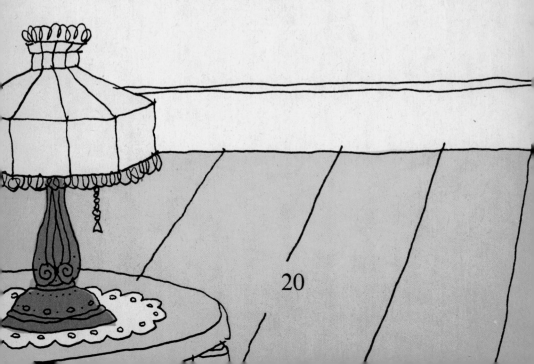

An open door

is a sign of friendship.

An open door says *Come in*."

Scarlet opened her door wide

and stood in front of it.

After a while she sat

in front of her open door.

At last she lay down

in front of her open door.

First she lay on her back.

Then she lay on her stomach.

Then she lay on her side.

26

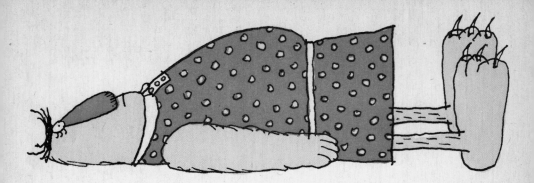

"Well," she said.

"The breeze is coming in,

and the smell of lilacs

is coming in,

and a stream of sunlight

is coming in.

But that is all

that is coming in."

Scarlet got up

and slammed her door shut.

Then she paced back and forth.

Suddenly she stopped.

"Scarlet Monster,

you are more than stupid,"

she said.

"You could win first prize

and a blue ribbon

in a stupid contest,

because you have not built

a cheerful fire

in your fireplace!"

Scarlet gathered wood.

"When my neighbors see smoke.

coming from my chimney,

they will certainly

rush to meet me,"

she thought.

Scarlet built a fire

in her fireplace.

"With a cheery fire

and brownies and beets

and me for company,

everyone will come," she said.

Scarlet toasted marshmallows

over her fire.

"Well," she thought,

"the rush is not rushing yet.

Maybe the smoke from my fire

cannot be seen

over the trees.

I have a better idea.

If my neighbors cannot see

that I am here,

they can hear

that I am here."

Scarlet went outside.

She opened her mouth

and sang in her loudest voice,

"EVERYONE

PLEASE COME AND MEET

THE BRAND-NEW MONSTER

ON YOUR STREET!"

Scarlet waited.

But all was quiet.

So she sang on,

"A CHEERY FIRE

AND LOTS OF TREATS,

HOME-BAKED BROWNIES,

PICKLED BEETS."

Scarlet sang so loud and so long

that her throat hurt.

38

She went back into her house.

She plopped into her easy chair.

"No one is coming," she said.

"and I know why.

Nobody likes me

because I am a monster.

They saw me and said,

'Look at that big klunk.

She weighs 300 pounds.

Her fangs need braces.

And her eyebrows look evil.' "

Scarlet started to cry.

"Nobody knows

that I think kind thoughts

and have a loving heart."

Scarlet looked at the pictures on her wall.

"Even for a monster,

I am ugly," she said. "Grandpa Monster

had soft white eyebrows.

Grandma Monster's fangs

were straight.

Mama and Papa

only weigh 235 pounds

and they do not *plop*

when they sit down."

Scarlet lapped her tears.

"I am the pits," she said.

"And nobody wants

to be friends with me.

That is bad. That is awful.

That is all the way down to

terrible.

It is so terrible

that I cannot think

my beautiful thoughts.

And right now I am thinking

the worst thoughts

I can think of.

I hate everybody."

Scarlet locked her door.

She pulled down her window shades.

She put out her fire.

"If my neighbors do not want me,

then I do not want them.

That makes it even," she said.

Scarlet plopped into her chair.

She sat there for a long time.

Then she said,

"My face is all sticky

from my tears.

And my mouth is all salty

and sad.

I need some fresh air."

Scarlet unlocked her door.

She went outside

and took a deep breath.

Then she walked down her front path

and along the street.

She saw someone come out

of a house

and walk toward her.

"I will hold my head

high in the air

and pass him by," thought Scarlet.

Scarlet raised her head high.

"Well, hello. I am Hugo!"

"I am a very beautiful monster,"

said Scarlet,

and she kept on walking.

Hugo turned and followed her.

"Are you happy in your new home?"

he asked.

"So what if my fangs need braces?"

said Scarlet,

and she walked on.

"Everyone in the neighborhood

wants to meet you,"

said Hugo.

"I am *proud*

of my evil-looking eyebrows,"

said Scarlet.

"Can we meet you now?" asked Hugo.

"I am truly *glad*

that I weigh 300 pounds,"

said Scarlet.

"Everyone is happy

that you live on our street,"

said Hugo.

"What?" asked Scarlet.

She stopped walking.

"Did you say *happy*?"

"Oh yes," said Hugo.

"But nobody knows me," said Scarlet.

"We looked in your window,"

said Hugo.

"We saw you baking brownies.

We saw you print and hang a sign.

We watched you paint your mailbox.

We saw you build a fire

in your fireplace.

We heard you sing songs.

Then we saw you resting

in your doorway."

"Oh," said Scarlet.

"Your brownies smelled delicious,"

said Hugo.

"Your song sounded sweet.

Your fire looked friendly."

"Oh my," said Scarlet.

"Then why didn't anyone

come to visit me?"

Hugo looked at his feet.

"We did not know," he said,

"if you would like

monsters like us."

"You mean you are really glad

I am here?" she asked.

"Sure," said Hugo.

"Oh," said Scarlet again.

"Then I am really glad

I am here."

She kissed Hugo.

Hugo kissed her back.

Somebody else came up

and kissed Scarlet.

And somebody else.

"And I am glad

this is a kissing neighborhood,"

said Scarlet.

"Now, everyone, please come

into my new house

for brownies and pickled beets."

And everyone did.